Storm Tide

Kari Jones

Orca currents

ORCA BOOK PUBLISHERS

Library and Archives Canada Cataloguing in Publication

Jones, Kari, 1966-
Storm tide / Kari Jones.
(Orca currents)

Issued also in electronic formats.
ISBN 978-1-55469-808-0 (bound).--ISBN 978-1-55469-807-3 (pbk.)

I. Title. II. Series: Orca currents
ps8619.05328S76 2011   jc813'.6   c2010-907952-3

First published in the United States, 2011
Library of Congress Control Number: 2010941955

Summary: Simon and his sister Ellen have to solve the mystery of the hidden treasure if they want to save the island lighthouse they call home.

Orca Book Publishers is dedicated to preserving the environment and has printed this book on paper certified by the Forest Stewardship Council.

Orca Book Publishers gratefully acknowledges the support for its publishing programs provided by the following agencies: the Government of Canada through the Canada Book Fund and the Canada Council for the Arts, and the Province of British Columbia through the BC Arts Council and the Book Publishing Tax Credit.

Cover design by Teresa Bubela
Cover photography by Getty Images

ORCA BOOK PUBLISHERS   ORCA BOOK PUBLISHERS
PO BOX 5626, Stn. B   PO BOX 468
Victoria, BC Canada   Custer, WA USA
V8R 6s4   98240-0468

www.orcabook.com
Printed and bound in Canada.

14 13 12 11 • 4 3 2 1

To Rowan and Michael,
the first adventurers.

Chapter One

Today is going to be great. I head down to the dock to wave goodbye to Mom and Dad. They're going to Victoria for the day. That means that apart from my sister Ellen, who doesn't really count, I am totally alone on the island for the whole day.

On my way back to the house, I plan my day. I can do whatever in the world

I want. I've lived on this island all twelve years of my life, and this is the first time I have been alone on it for an entire day. If it warms up, I'm going to swim in the water hole. Then I want to check out the spring salmon run off Rudlin Bay.

First I need a couple of sandwiches, one for right now and one to take with me. I'm going to start the day with a hike to the midden on the other side of the island. A midden is basically an ancient First Nations garbage dump. That sounds gross, but it's actually really cool. All the gross stuff has decomposed by now, and all that's left are shells and bones covering a long stretch of beach. I go over there sometimes and sift through it. I have a good collection of bones from that site. But first things first, it's time to head inside for a snack.

Unfortunately, as I pull the ham and cheese out of the fridge, Ellen walks in.

"What are you doing?" she asks.

Ellen's voice has this mocking edge that would normally tick me off, but the last thing I want today is to fight with her, so I answer simply, "Making a sandwich."

"I can see that, Simon, but why?" Ellen says. This time there's no ignoring the you-are-so-stupid tone in her voice.

"I'm hungry." *Duh!* I don't say that out loud. I don't want to risk my day of freedom, after all.

"*That* hungry?" she points to the huge amount of food.

You'd think she could figure it out, but I patiently explain that I'm making food to last a while.

"What about your chores?" she says.

"What about them?" I ask.

Ellen puts her hands on her hips and stands between me and the fridge. I'm uncomfortable with where this conversation is going. I don't want to fight with Ellen today, but I can see my plans for the day disappearing if I let her tell me what to do.

"Mom and Dad expect the chores to be done. We're the keepers while they're away. They've got enough to worry about. You are not going anywhere until you've done your chores."

I hate it when Ellen speaks to me like that. But I have to admit it's true. Mom and Dad have a hard day ahead of them. The government's been closing lighthouses all around here. Dad is sure Discovery Island Lighthouse Station is next. He and Mom are going to tell the people at the ministry about all the things they do: rescue boaters, keep weather records and help the biologists collect data on waves and currents. Man, I hope they can convince them that the lighthouse station should stay open. This is my *home*!

"I'll have lots of time for chores," I say. I start spreading mustard on the bread.

Ellen stands there and watches me. She looks so much like Mom right now. Mom doesn't have to say anything. She has this look. Ellen has it too. Someday my sister is going to make one scary mother. I look back at her, trying to ignore the Mom look, but it's useless. The look is working. I can feel it.

"Okay, okay, I'll do my chores first," I say.

"You'd better. Then you can do whatever you want." Ellen smiles sweetly.

Ha.

My main job is the boat shed. I keep it tidy so we can pull the boats in quickly during storms. I was rummaging in the shed looking for my fishing rod yesterday, so I know exactly how messy it is. This is going to take forever, half an hour at least!

I start with the ropes. I coil them properly and hang them in their spot on the wall. Then I organize the crab traps and the motor parts and oars and paddles and life jackets. After a while I start thinking that something feels different. I can't put my finger on what it is, but something is out of place. I feel like I've half noticed something, but it's taking a while to get into my brain. I look around. Everything looks the same, doesn't it? What's different?

I walk back to the entrance of the shed and look outside. Nope. Everything looks right there—the rubber tire that we use as a bumper on the dock, the bucket and hose we keep for rinsing salt water off our gear. There's a barrel of strawberries Mom planted to make the place prettier. I turn back to the shed and look around inside. Everything is in the shed that should be. Isn't it? Maybe it's just my imagination.

I put this thought out of my mind and finish cleaning. When I'm done, I step onto the wooden planks leading from the shed to the dock. And I figure out what is missing.

A chill creeps up my back. I swear, when I walked into this shed half an hour ago, there were muddy footprints on the dock. They aren't there now.

Chapter Two

The thing about a small island with only one lighthouse keeper and his family living on it is that anyone who comes to the island always stops in to say hello. Always.

That's why it is so weird that I saw footprints. No one has come to visit. If someone came to the island without visiting, it wouldn't be the end of the world.

It's strange but not illegal. I stop worrying. Besides, now that my chores are done, I can head off for the day.

At home, I wrap my sandwich and shove it into a small backpack with a water bottle. It is chilly outside, so I shuffle through the clothes on the floor in my bedroom until I find my old blue sweater. I stick it into the backpack, and I'm ready to head off.

As soon as I step outside, I let out a groan. In the short time it took me to grab my stuff, the weather has turned windy. That happens here a lot. Weather springs up out of nowhere. Today it's an enormous pain in the rear, because now I have to check outside the light tower to make sure nothing's been left lying around. Dad always sends us to check when a wind comes along, so I know it's what he would expect.

I consider letting Ellen deal with it, but I don't feel like facing her. And if anything did get lost in the wind, we'd be in trouble. I'd have to explain why I didn't check. With a sigh, I take the path toward the tower.

It's not far. If I walk fast, it only takes a minute.

There is a small hill between the house and the tower, so I don't see the gray tent until I'm almost walking into it. It's old-fashioned, with straight poles making an A shape. The door is open and flaps in the wind. There's stuff all around. A sleeping bag spills out the tent door onto the grass, and a bag of clothes lies half-opened beside it. On the other side of the tent is a campstove with a pot half-full of water. The wind has pinned a map of the area to the wall of the tent. I've never seen such a messy campsite.

"Hello?" I call. There's no answer. "Hello!" I poke my head inside the tent. It's empty. I stand up and cup my hands around my mouth. "Hello! Anyone here?"

I get no answer. I'm starting to feel strange about this. No one has ever set up a tent on the island without asking. When they do ask, Dad always sends them to the meadow on the other side of the island to sleep away from the bright light. Why would someone pitch their tent under the light? Why would they do it without asking? It's totally weird. And it's the second weird thing to happen today.

As I look around, I wonder if the tent belongs to the same person the footprints did? It would be weirder if two separate people were doing strange things on the island, so I'm going with the idea that it's the same person. I don't know why, but there's something creepy about this thought. Is this person trying to avoid us?

My good mood about the day evaporates.

It sure is windy now. There are whitecaps in the strait, and on the rocky side of the headland, spray spews off the rocks with every wave. There are even ruffles in the bay. With every gust of wind, a shrub near the tower rubs against the wall, making a sound like chalk on a blackboard. I shiver.

What if the owner of the tent got caught out in the strait when the wind came up? They'd be in big trouble now. I walk back to the tent and call out again.

"Hello. Anyone here?" I really hope someone is hiding in the trees and is going to answer. There's no answer. I turn around and head back home, worrying about the wind. What if someone is in trouble? What will we do? This is not how I planned to spend my day. Even though I hate to do it, I'm going to have to see what Ellen thinks about this.

As soon as I'm close to the house, I yell "Ellen!" as loudly as I can to be heard over the wind.

"I'm right here. You don't have to yell," she says from the kitchen doorway.

"I need you to come. I saw a tent and called out, but there was no answer. Someone may be in trouble."

She gives me a don't-make-fun-of-serious-things look and turns back to the kitchen, but I grab at her sleeve. "Ellen, remember, we're keepers today. Someone might need our help."

She looks into my eyes, checking that I'm not teasing her, then says, "For once you're right. We should look. Just give me a second. I'll get a sweater."

When Ellen is in her room, the VHF radio cackles.

"Discovery Light, Discovery Light, this is Discovery Keeper. Over.

It's Dad. I pick up the receiver and say, "This is Discovery Light. Hey, Dad. Over."

"Simon, I'm glad we got you." Dad's voice cracks over the line. "The wind has picked up quite a bit here. We'll be delayed coming home. We may be quite late. Is everything okay? Over."

I consider telling Dad what's going on, but I don't want to worry him. It's probably nothing anyway. I'm sure the person camped by the lighthouse is just a hiker passing through.

"Sure," I say. "Everything is okay. Over."

Chapter Three

Ellen stands right where the tent had been not five minutes ago and stares at me. "Weirdo," she says.

I have to admit, she's got a point. There's no tent here. Was I dreaming? I don't think so. I could swear there was a tent parked here just a few minutes ago. Didn't I shout out?

"It was here. It was. I'll prove it to you."

"Sure," snaps Ellen. "You're just doing this to get back at me about the chores. I know you." She's ready to stomp off back to the house, but I know the truth. Now I'm spooked. Disappearing muddy footprints are one thing. A disappearing tent is another.

"It was here. Really. Wait! Ellen, let me prove it to you."

I swivel my head around. There must be some evidence a tent was here a few minutes ago. The grass is chewed up from us walking over it every day, so I can't see exactly where the tent was. But there must be some way to prove I'm not going crazy or trying to get back at her.

The truth is, I'm beginning to wonder. Am I going crazy? What about the footprints? Same thing, I think. First they were there, and then they just…weren't. I need to prove that the tent was there. For myself, not just Ellen.

I get down onto my hands and knees and crawl around. Ellen stands with her arms crossed over her chest and glares at me. Her hair whips across her face in the wind, but she doesn't move. Any second now, she is going to say *hmph* and leave, but there must be something here. Something. If a person that messy had to pack up that quickly, they must have left something on the ground.

I sweep my hands over the grass and dirt, back and forth across the place where I think the tent was. My hands and knees are getting dirty, but I'm not finding anything.

I widen my search. There is a flat area right under the tower. I stand up and walk around it, looking carefully.

It's strange what you notice when you really look. There is a lot of old bird doo and signs of other animals here. I find tiny holes from mice or moles and itsy-bitsy pieces of leaves that ants have left behind. There are spiderwebs in the low branches of the shrubs. Any other day, this would fascinate me, but today I'm frustrated. I can't understand what is going on.

I keep my eyes open for a color or texture that isn't natural. Nature's colors are soft, and so are its shapes. Bright red or yellow or blue is usually plastic. A sharp edge is usually man-made.

Ellen isn't even bothering to scowl anymore. She's laughing—at me.

"Weirdo. Why would you want to pretend there was a tent here?" she says. But I know, know, *know* that I saw what I saw, so I keep looking.

Ellen walks away, but she doesn't go far.

I'm on my knees with my head close to the ground when at last I find something. Sunlight glints off something shiny. I keep the spot in my sights as I stand up and walk to it. A tent peg lies at the edge of the spot I thought the tent was pitched. Next to the tent peg is a curious stone. I pick it up. It has numbers carved into it on one side and a flower like a rose on the other.

"Ellen, look." I'm almost jumping, I'm so excited. "Look, a tent peg. It must belong to that tent. Dad never lets anyone camp here. See? And this too, whatever it is." I hold the peg and the stone up for her to look at, but she is distracted.

"Simon, look. What's that?" Ellen points out to the bay.

"What are you looking at?"

"Out there. What is it?"

We peer out at the bay. The wind is getting stronger and stronger on the headland. It's hard to keep our hair out of our eyes. But there is something out there in the water. What is it?

Chapter Four

"Simon, it's a head. Someone's in the water!" says Ellen.

She's right. Where the bay ends and the rocks begin, a head is bobbing around in the waves. Then I see a small rowboat listing badly in the middle of the bay.

"They've fallen out of their boat," I say. I turn to look at Ellen. Her eyes are big and round, like mine feel. We are thinking the same thing.

Ellen whispers, "We're the keepers today."

"We have to help him," I whisper back.

Without talking, we spin around and run to the boathouse. I stuff the tent peg and stone into my pocket.

Thank goodness it's not too windy in the bay, because Mom and Dad have the big motorboat. Ellen and I are going to have to row. We've been in the rowboat a million times, in the bay and all around the island, but rowing is a lot of work. Just what we need. We'll have to stay inside the bay and out of the wind.

"Take these." Ellen hands me life jackets and our life-saving ring. I put on a life jacket and throw the rest of the stuff into the boat.

"Some rope too," I say, grabbing the rope off the wall. I'm glad I'd done my chores in the shed. We can actually find things. Together, Ellen and I push the boat into the water and settle onto the seats.

The first three or four strokes are fine, but as soon as we are away from the boat shed and the protection of the shore, I realize it's way windier in the bay than I'd thought. I grunt as I pull on the oars. Ellen stands up, one hand on the gunwale, and pulls the hair off her face. Salt spray lands on my arms.

In a rowboat, the person rowing is facing backward to where they are going, and the person not rowing faces toward where they are going. When Ellen and I go out together, I usually row first and she navigates, then after a while we switch.

"I can't see the head anymore," she shouts to be heard over the wind. "The wind is picking up way faster than I'd expected. Maybe we should just turn around."

I nod my head because already I am finding it hard to keep the boat moving in the direction I want to go. Turning around seems like an excellent idea.

Until I try. As soon as I sweep the oar to change the angle of the boat, I know it's going to be impossible. The boat tilts dangerously to the left, and water slops over the side. It slides around the bottom of the boat, wetting my toes.

"I can't turn around. The wind's too strong." My voice sounds panicky.

"Aim for the far shore," Ellen says, and she slides in beside me. I let her have the starboard oar, and I put all my weight into pulling the port one.

I can't believe we've been this stupid. You'd think living here all our lives, we'd know better. But that's the thing with wind and waves: you often can't tell how strong they are until you're in them. We pull and pull on the oars, but as hard as we pull, we can't escape the waves. I look over my shoulder.

We're being pushed out to sea.

"Pull harder," I yell at Ellen. Both of us tense and pull, tense and pull. Slowly, the bow of the boat shifts, and then our angle swings around. Water spills over the gunwales, but we stay upright. Now we're heading toward the far shore. There's no time to take a breath. We have to keep rowing, or we'll lose our angle and head back out to sea. Up and down the waves we ride. Up and down and up and down.

I've given up finding the person in the water when Ellen yells, "Look, there!" The man—we can see he has a beard—is on the surface, but is clearly struggling. I watch out of the corner of my eye, since I don't dare turn around. He keeps disappearing under the water for long periods.

"We can't reach him," says Ellen, and I nod. But I see him surface again.

For a second, I look right into his face. We lock eyes, and I feel a jolt of the man's terror all down my back.

With a new burst of strength, I pull my oar to change the angle of the boat. It is just enough to send us past the man.

"What are you doing?" Ellen yells.

I ignore her and pull again. The boat shifts more, and we hurtle along a wave, heading right for the man in the water.

"You hold the boat steady," I call to Ellen. She opens her mouth, but doesn't say anything. I hand her my oar and slide across, reaching under a seat for the lifes-aving ring. I check the rope on the ring, then tie the other end of the rope to my seat.

"One, two, three," I say, and I fling the ring overboard. It lands far from the man. I brace myself and pull on the rope to bring the life-saving ring back in. I try again. This time I risk crouching over so I can get a better angle. Again, the ring lands too far from the man. As I sit back down, a wave sloshes over the gunwale, soaking Ellen and me. The wind is getting worse.

"One last try." I grit my teeth. If I mess this one up, this guy's going to drown. This time I sit low, my knees resting on the bottom of the boat. I swing the rope as hard as I can and hope.

The ring lands right on top of the man's head. For a second it looks like it is going to slide off, but then it sinks over his neck.

"Hurrah," says Ellen in a strained voice.

She keeps pulling on the oars while I pull on the rope. I have to go gently so the ring won't come off the man's neck. He's heavy, and I have to lean back to pull him closer. After a minute of pulling, I've got him alongside the boat.

"Is he alive?" asks Ellen.

Chapter Five

"I can't tell." I reach over to grab him under the arms so I can hoist him in, but the boat lists too far. We almost go over. Quickly, I pull back.

"You'll have to brace on the other side," I yell at Ellen. She slides over so that all her weight is on the opposite side of the boat. She leans as far over the other side as she can while still holding on to both oars.

I try again. This time I manage to get my arms under the man without tipping the boat, but he is heavy. I almost drop him. I try a third time, and slowly his head and then his shoulders slide out of the water. I can hold him above water, but I can't pull him up any farther.

"Ellen, let the gunwale dip further," I yell. She leans her weight back toward the center of the boat. With a huge groan and all the strength I can find, I pull. The boat lists dangerously, but I lift the man until I can pull his head and shoulders into the boat.

"Quick," yells Ellen, as the boat takes on water. Together we grab at the man's coat and slide him on board. He takes up most of the bottom of the boat. Ellen turns his face out of the water so that he can breathe.

"Get into the seat," shouts Ellen. "Grab an oar." She doesn't have to say it twice. If we don't get this boat under control, we're all going over.

We tense and pull, tense and pull, tense and pull. The boat bounces on the waves. We can't gain control. "There's too much water in here."

Ellen hands me her oar and fumbles for the scoop under the seat. She finds it and starts bailing water. There is a ton of water in the boat, but she gets most of it out. Now the boat is easier to control. When she returns to the seat, I let her take an oar.

Tense and pull, tense and pull, tense and pull. These are my only thoughts, my only actions. I'm too tired to think about the man at the bottom of the boat.

It feels like hours later when we finally reach the shelter of the land. The wind and waves drop away. I let go of my oar and fall forward. Every muscle in my body screams at me as I let the boat drift onto the shore. It crunches onto the rocky beach, and Ellen and I crawl out. With the man on the bottom, the boat is as heavy as a yacht, and Ellen and I struggle to pull it up so it won't float away with the tide. Both of us collapse back onto the beach.

The beach never felt so wonderful. Every rock reminds me I am safe. "Aghhh…" is the only thing I can say as I lie there breathing.

Then Ellen says, "What's that noise?"

I sit up. "Noise?"

"Listen."

There are seagulls, as always, screeching overhead. The trees creak in the wind, and the sea scratches at the rocks on the beach as it surges. But these sounds are always here. Then I hear something else.

"It's the man. He's moaning." Ellen and I are up and looking over the gunwale of the boat in a second.

My heart pounds fast. The man hasn't moved, but he is making noise.

"He's alive!" says Ellen. We smile at each other in relief.

We manage to pull the man out of the boat. He opens his eyes for a second and moans.

"Hey, are you okay?" I ask.

He doesn't answer. His body goes limp, and we have to put our arms around his waist and half carry, half drag him onto the trail. It's too narrow for the three of us, so we walk sideways in single file with me in front, then the man, then Ellen. Normally it takes ten minutes to walk from the far side of the bay to the boat shed. Today it takes ages. Every few seconds we have to stop to rest. I am panting and soaked through with sweat. I've never felt so hungry in my life. All I want is to reach home and hand this man over to Mom and Dad. I don't even have the energy to talk.

When we emerge from the bush and see the boat shed ahead of us, I say, "Oh no!" Mom and Dad aren't back. The shed is just as we left it. There's no motorboat.

"I thought they'd be back by now," says Ellen, sounding like she is about to cry.

We lower the man onto the ground and stand there with our arms hanging loose. Neither of us moves.

"What should we do?" says Ellen. She looks exhausted. She must be, if she's asking for my advice. But I'm exhausted too, so I just shake my head.

The man moans again, and I take a deep breath and pull myself together. "We have to get him inside. He's soaked. He needs to get warm." Ellen nods. We pick him up and start walking again, this time a little faster.

Inside, we head straight for the sofa. We bend down and let the man fall onto the seat. He slides down so that he is lying across the cushions. He lies there for a second, then turns over and throws up.

"Ohhhh…gross," I say. The salty stink of it fills the air. I think I am going to be sick myself, so I run out of the room. I calm myself and head for the radio to call the coast guard.

"Discovery Lighthouse to coast guard, come in. Over." I say.

No answer.

"Discovery Lighthouse to coast guard, come in. Over."

"We read you, Discovery Lighthouse. Simon, how's it going over there? Over."

"Mark, is that you?" I ask. "We need you to send an ambulance."

"Are you two okay?"

"We're okay, but we hauled some guy out of the water. He needs to get to the hospital. Can you send an ambulance?"

"No can do, kiddo. Can't send anyone out in weather like this. Where is he now?"

"We've got him here with us. In the living room."

"Keep him warm. We'll send someone when it calms down."

I slowly put down the handset.

I try Mom and Dad on the boat, but I don't really expect them to answer. There's no way they would be out in this weather. We don't have landlines or cell phones on the island. I keep bugging Mom about it, but so far she hasn't budged on the issue. Too expensive, she says. If only she knew what was happening now.

I walk back to the living room. Ellen is cleaning up the mess with one hand and pinching her nose with the other. She looks up at me. "When will they get here?" she asks.

I shrug. "Mark says they can't send someone in this weather."

"Mom and Dad?"

"No answer."

Ellen's whole body sags. We look at the man lying on the sofa. He's breathing, but he looks unconscious. Then Ellen looks at me. "What are we going to do?"

Chapter Six

Ellen drops the rag into the bucket and stands up. She runs the back of her hand across her eyes. I think she's about to lose it, but she takes a deep breath, puts her hands in prayer position and closes her eyes. She takes a deep breath. "It's okay," she says. "We can deal with this. Look at you. You're shivering. Go upstairs and change out of those wet clothes.

I'll do the same, and then we'll make some tea. We'll make some extra in case he wakes up. It will warm him up. But first, let's prop up his head in case he needs to throw up again."

Wow. I'm impressed. Not that I'd ever tell Ellen, but what she just did was totally cool. Hearing her take control makes me feel calm. I nod and grab a pillow from the armchair while Ellen lifts the man's head. I place the pillow under him and throw a blanket over him. Then I run upstairs and change.

After we've had some hot tea, I feel better. I have stopped shivering, but now I'm starting to feel nervous again. I don't like the look of this man. His beard is ragged, and his shoes have holes in them. I can't help wondering what he was doing out on the water in such bad weather. Why did he pitch that tent without asking? And why did he take it down so suddenly? What is he doing here?

A branch of the tree growing next to the house hits the wall. That's some wind out there. I shiver. The lights flicker, then go out. It's only three o'clock, but the sky is very dark from the storm. With the power out, the house is dark.

"Oh no." Ellen looks out the window.

I don't have to ask what she's thinking. There's no way Mom and Dad are out in the boat in this wind.

"They're not going to get home soon, are they?" I ask. Ellen shakes her head. I close my eyes and take a ragged breath. This is *so* not the day I was hoping for.

Ellen and I take turns sitting with the man. He lies there, snoring sometimes. When it's my turn, I light as many candles as I can to brighten the room, and I pull the armchair close to the couch so that I can see if he's breathing.

I try to read my book, but I'm so tired that I nod off sitting in the armchair. I wake with a start when I hear talking. It's the man.

I sit upright and shake my head to clear my mind. Then I lean over so that I can hear what he's saying. The candles have almost all burned out, so I can just make out his face. His eyes are closed. He's talking in his sleep.

"Gerhe trtre trea sureofjuan fuca…"

"What?" I whisper.

"Trtre trea sureofjuan fuca," he says again.

Am I hearing right? Fuca what? I almost giggle. Puka? Does he want to puke again? Or is he trying to say something else?

Ellen's asleep in the other chair. I poke her shin with my foot. "Wake up."

She opens her eyes, then straightens up. "What?"

I point to the man. "Listen."

We wait. In a few minutes, he says it again.

"Trtre trea sureofjuan fuca…"

"Huh?" The look on her face makes me laugh. She laughs too. Soon we are laughing so hard, we can't stop.

"Fuca, fuca, fuca," he calls out.

That gets us laughing again, but our laughter is close to crying. Both of us are feeling tired and crazy.

Chapter Seven

Ellen takes a turn watching the man, so I go to bed for a while, even though it's only about six o'clock. I fall asleep so fast, I don't even have time to pull down the covers. But soon Ellen is waking me up.

"Hurry," she says and runs out of the room. I am instantly awake, my heart pounding. I remember everything about the day. The tent, the boat ride, the man. Oh no, what's happened now?

Ellen is standing behind the armchair in the living room, and the man is pacing between the chairs and sofa. With each step he flings his arms in the air.

"Calm down," she says.

He ignores her. "I have to get it. Where's my bag? NOW!" he shouts.

"Get what?" I ask. He spins around to look at me.

"Oh good, you're here. I figured it out. The riddle, the map. It all makes sense now."

Is he talking to me?

"What do you mean?" I ask.

"De Fuca's treasure. It all makes sense now." He leans in close to me and whispers, "It's taken me a year to translate that riddle. I'm not missing this chance. De Fuca's treasure!" He lurches forward and grabs my collar. "WHERE IS MY BAG?" I pull back, wrenching my shirt free. He turns after me as I run around the chair to the other side of the room. "MY BAG," he shouts again. I run over to Ellen, and we huddle behind the armchair.

"He's hallucinating. He thinks I'm someone else," I whisper to Ellen.

"No kidding," she whispers back.

He lunges toward us. I can feel Ellen trembling, so I push her behind me and step in front of the chair. "What kind of treasure is it? What riddle are you talking about?"

The man stops and peers down his nose at me. For a second he looks like he's going to get crazy again, but then he sways and reaches out to steady himself. Slowly, he sinks onto the sofa and lies back. His body shivers for a few seconds, but then he's still. I bend over and snap my fingers in his face, but he doesn't respond. Ellen lets out a loud breath behind me.

"That was scary," she says.

"Yeah, no kidding."

Ellen's whole body is shaking as she lowers herself into the armchair. "You were cool, Simon. Standing up to him like that."

I'd never admit it to her, but hearing those words makes me happy. "Thanks," I say. I bend over the man again and snap my fingers just to make sure he's passed out. Nothing. Nothing at all. Is he even breathing? The last thing we need now is for him to stop breathing. I put my ear to his mouth. A puff of air hits my ear. He's breathing.

I look at Ellen. "Do you think he's in trouble?" I ask.

"I think we'd better find this tent of his and see if his bag is in it," she says.

"So you believe me now, do you?" I ask.

Ellen begins to give me one of her looks, but then she says, "He might have some ID in there. He's not looking good, and I want to be able to tell the ambulance guys who he is."

"When we get an ambulance," I say glumly.

"Yeah."

I stand up and look out the window. It's still really windy, and it's totally dark. Our options are to stay inside with a crazy man, who may or may not start hallucinating again, or to go outside and look for a tent. I look longingly at the radio, but I know that no one is coming any time soon. Not Mom and Dad, not the coast guard—no one.

I nod. "Let's go. The less time I have to spend with this man, the better."

We put on warm coats and grab flashlights. When Ellen opens the door, it swings wide open and the wind hits us. We struggle up the path and over the short hill until we are facing the light tower. As soon as we see it, we both stop. Ellen turns to me.

"Uh-oh."

I know exactly what she means. In all the excitement, neither of us remembered that we were supposed to check the barometer, make sure the rain meter was okay, take a look at the sunshine recorder and check that the light was working properly.

"We'd better go in and check things. Then we'll look for the tent," I say. Ellen nods, and we head to the tower.

The wind is so strong that it takes both of us to open the door. We grab the handle and pull. At first it won't open at all, but once we get it open a crack, it swings wide. We tumble inside and pull the door closed behind us.

We race up the spiral staircase and look around. The tower light is fueled by diesel, so even when the power goes out, it still works. Things seem to be okay up here. It only takes us a few minutes to check the barometer and thermometer and write out a weather report for Dad to send in the morning.

We climb back down the stairs more slowly.

"Now we have to figure out where the tent is. How are we going to find it in the middle of a storm?" I have hardly said these words when I see something beside the stairs.

I swing my flashlight over to take a closer look. Gray fabric. I bend over and pull it out. The tent!

The man has left it in a heap. Ellen pulls one end and I pull the other until we find the door. The space at the bottom of the stairs is too small to spread the tent out, so I'm going to have to crawl inside it to take a look.

"What a mess," says Ellen. "How could he leave his tent like this? What was he thinking?"

"Here goes," I say as I shove my head in the door hole. Once I'm, in I stand up, using my arms to hold up the sides. Ellen shines her flashlight through the doorway so I can see. There's a pile of clothes and a sleeping bag in the center, so I shuffle my feet around them a bit, but there doesn't seem to be anything interesting there. Right beside the door is a small mesh pocket with a plastic bag in it. I bend over and pull the bag out.

"Shine your flashlight over here," I call out. Ellen's head appears in the doorway, and she shines her flashlight on my hands. I open the bag. Inside is a small leather pouch, which I open too. Inside that are two pieces of paper. One is a handwritten letter.

The other is a map.

Chapter Eight

I crawl out of the tent so we can take a look at the papers. We start by opening the map. I flatten it against my leg and hold it up so both of us can take a look. The map is about the size of a newspaper, and it's old, judging by the curled edges. It looks like it was drawn by hand. There is a big island in the center, with a bunch of smaller islands and very tiny ones around its edges. Some of the lines are smudged, like the map got wet at some point. A lot of the image is faded, and down the center is a hole where the paper has worn away from being folded so many times. The words on the map are in some language we can't understand. There's only one word we recognize: *Fuca*.

"Like the explorer?" I ask.

Ellen shrugs. "I guess."

"Hey, it's our island. Look." I trace my finger across the outline of the island.

"Hang on," I say, and I rush back to the top of the tower and grab a pen and paper.

"Hold the map against the wall," I tell Ellen when I get back. I put the flashlight in my mouth and place a sheet of paper over the old map.

"Slow down," says Ellen. She's right. My hands are shaking, so I slow down and start again.

It's a lot easier to see on the new sheet of paper. "Yes, this is definitely the island. Look, here's the bay, here's the headland. Here are the little islands off the coast." I tap the paper with my finger.

It seems weird though. Most people, when they make maps, include as much information as they can, things like roads or forests or mountains. There's none of that stuff here. This is just an outline of the island with a little circle near where the light tower is.

We stare at each other. "Let's look at the letter," Ellen says. She takes it from me and opens it up. She spreads it out on the wall, and I shine my flashlight on it. The paper is newer, but the letter has also been wet at some point. I can hardly read it. I copy what I can onto my own paper. I read aloud:

The tide will hide what seekers seek,
Till stars will climb out from the deep.

Your heading from the star to make;
De Fuca's loot, yours soon to take.

"Huh?" says Ellen. "Fuca again? I bet this is a translation of what's on the other paper."

"Yeah…but what is it about?"

Ellen shakes her head. "I don't know. It's all totally confusing."

I take a deep breath. "Yeah," I say. "Who writes stuff like this?"

"Someone who wants to hide something, I'd say," says Ellen.

"So what are they hiding, and where?" Neither of us has the answers to those questions. I fold the letter and the map and put them back into the leather pouch. As I slide them in, I feel something else in the pouch.

"Shine that flashlight over here," I say.

"What is it?"

"His ID. His name is Joseph Edison. He's a member of the Royal Historical

Society, whatever that is." I look at Ellen. "Now we know his name, but what on earth is he doing here?"

"I don't know."

Somehow knowing his name makes him a little less creepy. I take the pouch and put it back in the plastic bag, and put the plastic bag back in the tent.

"What should we do with this?" I say holding up a corner of the tent.

"Let's just leave it," says Ellen. "He can tidy it up and take it away in the morning."

"Wow, Ellen, leave a mess?" There are all kinds of possibilities for teasing here.

She kicks lamely at the wall and says, "It's too frustrating." I decide to stop teasing her.

Instead, I glance down at the sheet of paper still in my hand. The lines of the riddle stare back at me. And then I notice:

De Fuca's loot, yours soon to take.

"De Fuca's loot," I say. "That must mean something about Juan de Fuca, the explorer. *Your heading from the star to make*. That makes sense. It's saying take a heading from a star to point out which direction to look. And what's the brightest star around?" I tilt my head to look up at the light at the top of the tower. Ellen follows my gaze.

"The tower light," we say together.

As we say that, an idea sparks at the back of my brain. I'm not going to say anything yet, because the idea is only a small leaf curled up in my mind.

Chapter Nine

I don't think either of us has ever made it up those stairs so quickly. If we can take a heading from the light, we may be able to understand the riddle. As I race to the top, I remember what the man said. He used the word *treasure*. Could he mean Juan de Fuca's treasure? I wrack my brains to think if I have ever heard about Juan de Fuca having some connection to treasure around here. Nothing comes to mind. As far as I know, he never even came down Juan de Fuca Strait. They named it after him because he was the first European to sail across the top of it and recognize it for what it was. That's all. This is all probably just a bunch of hooey.

At the top of the stairs, we walk onto the observation deck and stare out into the night. The light sweeps over the rocks, revealing every crag and outcrop as it goes. As it passes over the ocean, we see whitecaps on the waves. We turn to the back of the observation deck to watch the light sweep across the island and over the strait. It's a beautiful sight that I never get tired of, but tonight it's not what I want to see.

I look at Ellen. "If we had thought for one second, we would have known this light couldn't be the star. It shines on everything in sight. You can't take a heading from a moving light."

"Yeah. It could be any one of those rocks or coves or anything out there." She leans out over the railing, but the wind is too strong and she quickly pulls herself back.

When we get back to the house, the man—Joseph—is still asleep on the couch. His clothing is all rumpled, and he's snoring away, but I'm worried that he'll wake up and start shouting again.

"I think we should tie him up or something," I say to Ellen, who is also looking at him a bit fearfully.

"No way," she says.

"Why not?" It seems like a perfectly good idea to me, but Ellen glares at me and says, "We are not tying anybody up. That would make us kidnappers. What are you thinking?"

I shrug my shoulders. "I wasn't thinking about kidnapping. I just don't want him to wake up and go bonkers on us again."

"I have a better idea," says Ellen, and she walks out of the room. I follow her into Mom and Dad's room. Once we are both inside, she closes the door and turns the key. "We'll lock ourselves in. That way we're not kidnapping him, but we're safe."

This is twice tonight that Ellen has been brilliant. I smile at her. "Good thinking, Ellen."

"Thank you," she says.

I take off my shoes and pants and lie in Mom and Dad's big bed. Ellen slips into the bathroom and comes back wearing one of Mom's nightgowns, then slides in beside me. It's weird to be in here with her, but we're safe and warm. I don't think about it for more than the half a second it takes me to fall asleep.

I wake with a start. Dawn light is coming in through the window. The first thing that pops into my mind is that Mom and Dad will be home any minute. The second thing that reaches its way in is the sound of wind.

I can't believe the storm is still going. If it's still windy at the house, then the strait is likely impassable. Mom and Dad won't be on their way home yet. Will this storm never end?

I shake Ellen until she opens her eyes. "We should check on Joseph."

"Go ahead," she mumbles and rolls over. She burrows deeper under the covers. But I don't want to go alone. The truth is, I'm scared. After he freaked out on us last night, I don't want to face him alone. I shake Ellen again.

This time she looks at me blankly for a second. Then her eyes clear and she sits up. "Joseph. The ambulance."

"Not here yet. It's still stormy." I pull on my pants and shove my feet into my shoes. I unlock the door, but I wait for Ellen to pull on Mom's housecoat and follow me before I leave the room.

We walk down the stairs together. I'm listening for noises—snoring, rustling, anything to tell us if he's awake, asleep, alive. At the bottom of the stairs, I stop so suddenly that Ellen bumps into me.

Where Joseph had been sleeping, there is just a rumpled sofa and a half-empty glass of water.

He's gone.

Chapter Ten

Ellen sinks into the nearest armchair. Relief, confusion, frustration and fear all flit across her face. I'm not too sure about this either. I mean, sure, I am happy to not have a semi-drowned, deranged, potentially dangerous man in my living room. I am totally, totally happy about that. But...where is he? And what is he doing? Is he really okay?

Should we worry about him or be glad he's gone?

Plus, there is that small thought in the back of my brain. It has been rattling about in there, not quite forming into an idea, but I know it's important. I close my eyes and sit. Here's my thought. What if Joseph is looking for treasure that really exists? I mean, that's really treasure, not just some kooky man's idea of treasure. What if it is actually treasure from Juan de Fuca? I mean gold and silver and jewels. What if Ellen and I find it? Could we save the lighthouse? Could we save our home?

To find the treasure, we need Joseph. So yeah, I'm glad he's gone. And I'm not glad. I want a chance to save the lighthouse station.

I give a big, frustrated sigh.

Ellen looks over. "What?"

So I tell Ellen my thought. For a second she looks unimpressed. Then her eyebrows rise in an "aha" kind of look, and she says,

"Simon, we don't need the man. We've got a copy of his map and the riddle."

She's right!

Even in the light of day, the riddle makes no sense. We stare at it and repeat it to ourselves over and over.

The tide will hide what seekers seek,
Till stars will climb out from the deep.
Your heading from the star to make;
De Fuca's loot, yours soon to take.

I feel like my head is about to burst open from staring and thinking so much.

"Argh…what on earth can it mean?" I ask. "The only line that makes any sense at all is the last one. And if that means what I think it means…"

"Then it's important that we figure out the rest of it," Ellen ends the sentence for me.

"Exactly."

I sit there, my head in my hands, my brain totally blank. I hear the screech of seagulls and the morning chorus of birds as the daylight grows stronger. The wind isn't blowing as hard as it was last night. The tree has stopped scratching against the wall. Is the storm coming to an end at last?

"I'm going to go check on the dock," I say. All this sitting around isn't doing any good. Maybe doing something will help clear my brain.

"I'll come with you," says Ellen.

I'm relieved that she's coming, because Joseph must be out there somewhere. I don't want to find myself alone with him.

Outside, Ellen walks so close behind me that she's almost stepping on my heels. Any other day it would be annoying, but today I'm comforted by her presence. Tree branches and leaves are strewn everywhere from the storm. It's hard to move fast when you're snapping your head around at every sound in case someone else is on the trail. So we walk more slowly than usual down to the dock.

When we get there, I notice two things at once. First, the wind is dying down in the strait. Mom and Dad are likely on their way home. The other thing I notice is that the tide is low, and the rocks are covered in sea stars.

All that poring over the riddle pays off. I turn and yell "Ellen! Check it out!"

"Why are you screaming?" she says from right behind my elbow.

"I've solved part of the riddle. Look." I point at the sea stars all over the rocks.

She frowns. "What?"

"Listen: *The tide will hide what seekers seek / Till stars will climb out from the deep.*"

"Yeah?" she says, still not getting it.

"Look at the tide. It's so low. And look at the sea stars."

The next moment we are flying past the dock and onto the tidal flats. Ellen grabs me around the waist and hugs me until I can hardly breathe. "The tide hides the sea stars until a really low tide," she says. "Simon, you are a genius." She grins, and I grin back at her. "Whatever we are looking for is in the intertidal zone."

"The *low* part of the intertidal zone," I correct her.

There's a lot of grinning going on right now. We have just become treasure hunters!

Chapter Eleven

We rush to the other side of the bay, pushing each other in our hurry. The boat is where we left it in the grass above the beach. My stomach does a funny turnover at the thought of what Dad would say if he knew we'd left it here overnight in a storm. I never gave the boat a second's thought after we rescued Joseph. I push thoughts about Joseph right out of my head. He's probably holed up in his tent somewhere. I am not going to worry about him.

Ellen and I grab life jackets from the bottom of the boat and pull them on. Mine is still wet from last night, but I don't care. We pull the boat across the mudflat. When we reach the water, we slide into our usual positions, with me rowing and Ellen navigating.

Because the tide is so low, we are already far out in the bay. The rocks on the far side of the bay are covered in purple and orange sea stars. As we get close, I stop rowing and let the boat glide. All around the rocks, sea stars glisten in the sun. Ellen and I look at each other.

"Hmmm," says Ellen.

"Yeah, hmmm," I reply. Almost every rock is covered in sea stars. How on earth would we know which one to look at?

Ellen laughs. Her laughter sounds close to crying. "Of course, we are such idiots. We don't even know when the map was made. Sea stars don't sit on one rock forever." She looks around. "But you know, I think we got part of it right. I mean, the line *the tide will hide what seekers seek*—that still makes sense, right?"

"Yeah," I say slowly, "but that doesn't help us much." I row the boat to the dock, where we can sit and talk this through.

"Let's look again." I pull the copies of the map and the letter from my pocket and lay them out on my lap.

"It hardly looks like anything," I say, tracing the outline of the map with my finger. "So little detail. Why would they have so little detail?"

Ellen shrugs. "I don't know. Unless they were in a hurry. Or…maybe they didn't want other people to use the map."

"I know, it's so weird. It's like something is missing." And then I know.

That is exactly right. Something *is* missing.

"Let's start from the beginning," I say. I'm getting excited again. "First there were the disappearing muddy footprints."

"You didn't tell me about that."

"Here at the dock. First they were there, and then they were gone."

"On the dock?"

"Yeah. Then there was a disappearing tent. When we looked around, I found a tent peg AND..." I shouted, as a realization hit me, "and the painted stone. I forgot about it. When you saw Joseph out in the water, I just shoved the stone into my pocket. It must still be there."

Ellen is looking at me like I've lost my mind. "What stone?"

I take a deep breath. "Yesterday, when we went to look for the tent,

I found a little stone. I tried to show you, but you were already looking at Joseph in the water."

"Okay, yeah, but so what?"

"So…maybe the stone gives us the clue to the map. Maybe it fits with the riddle."

Chapter Twelve

We pull the boat onto shore and leave the oars inside so it'll be ready when we come back. At the house, I run upstairs and kick my way through the clothes on the floor until I find the pants I was wearing when we rescued Joseph. They're still soaking wet, and they cling to my fingers as I try to get my hand in the pocket. Then I feel the small round rock.

"Got it!" I holler and run downstairs.

"Wait," says Ellen. "Let's look here, where we can spread everything out. It'll be easier to see."

That makes sense, so I pull the copy of the map out of my pocket and lay it and the stone on the table. The stone has a pattern on one side that looks familiar. I think I should know what it is, but I can't quite get it. Is it a flower? A rose? There's a series of numbers on the other side of the stone.

Ellen leans over the table. "*Your heading from the star to make*—how can that be anything but the lighthouse? Unless it's a real star."

"Let's hope not. How would we figure out which one? Anyway, you don't make headings from a star unless you are out at sea. And they haven't done that for, like, a hundred years anyway. We take headings with charts, compasses…wait." I close my eyes and bring my hands up to my temples. "Ellen, think. Did I copy everything from the original map? Is there anything missing here?"

She looks over my shoulder at the map I drew. "It's hard to remember, but I don't think anything's missing. Why?"

I don't answer. Instead, I make myself walk calmly to Dad's office. I pull out one of the charts of Discovery Island and the area around it. Charts are like maps, but they are for boaters. They show water features like tides and currents. I walk back to Ellen and spread the chart out on the table. My hands are shaking with the effort to not rush.

It's hard to believe Dad's chart and the old map are of the same place. Our modern chart has squiggly blue lines marking sea depth, arrows pointing out boating lanes and colorful shapes marking lights and buoys. In the center there's a compass, so you can tell which way is north. There are even contour lines of the land.

"Look," I say.

"I am looking. Tell me." She leans over the map, her forehead creased in concentration.

"If we wanted to take a reading off this," I say, pointing to the chart from Dad's office, "we'd know exactly how to position our compass, wouldn't we?"

"Yeah."

"But how would we take a reading off this one?" I tap my hand-drawn map.

Now Ellen sees what I am getting at. She stands upright.

"There's nothing telling us which way is north," Ellen says.

"Exactly. And we never noticed, because we know this area so well. But if you were just arriving here, this map wouldn't mean anything."

"And," Ellen says, "there are no lines of latitude and longitude. Even if there were, we still wouldn't know which way was north."

"So there must be a clue somewhere else then. Some numbers. Like…" I pick up the stone and toss it in my hand. It lands upside down. A row of numbers stare back at me: *48 25 30 123 13 30*. Carefully, slowly, I place the stone on the table next to the map. "…these ones."

Ellen sits down heavily, and her jaw drops open. She says, "Degrees, minutes and seconds. Two sets of them, latitude and longitude. That makes it 48 degrees, 25 minutes and 30 seconds north. 123 degrees, 13 minutes and 30 seconds west."

"Yeah." I do a silly dance. I can't help it. I'm so excited, and I have to release the energy somehow.

But Ellen is still talking. "That's what those numbers say. At least I think they do. They could do." She's yelling now, she's so excited. She hops up and joins me in my dance. "Let's lay the old map on top of Dad's," she says.

I stop dancing and take a deep breath to slow myself down. Carefully I lift the piece of paper and lay it over Dad's chart. It's not a perfect fit, but it's pretty close. The rocks off the lighthouse are in the right spot, and the bay is in the right spot too.

Ellen hops from foot to foot until she can't contain herself anymore. Then she reaches over the table and helps me adjust the charts. I take a kitchen knife and use its edge as a ruler to measure out the longitude and latitude on Dad's chart. Ellen mutters as I go: "Okay, 48 degrees, 25 minutes and 30 seconds north. 123 degrees, 13 minutes and 30 seconds west."

When I'm done, I frown. "Well, that's no good. The spot is on land, up by the lighthouse."

"That doesn't make sense. The riddle said it should be in the intertidal zone." Ellen puts her finger on the riddle.

"And why would it have anything to do with the tide if it's there?"

We are silent as we try to sort out the puzzle.

"No," Ellen says. She jumps up and down and claps her hands like a little kid. "This is where the heading starts, not where it ends."

"What do you mean, where it starts?"

"With a compass, you need a starting point to take a heading from. Usually a headland or something."

"Oh." A thought jumps into my head. "That's where the star comes in: *Your heading from the star to make.*"

"Yes, yes, but what's the *star*?"

The silence lengthens as we try to make sense of this.

We are about to lose hope again. I close my eyes and think about everything we know. Something in the back of my brain slides forward, something I have known all along and didn't see. I turn over the stone. It flips with a small thud. And at last I know. The star.

I hold my palm out.

"The star," Ellen shouts. The center of the stone is painted in sixteen points: an old-fashioned compass star, not a flower. It's more elaborate than modern compasses. That's why we didn't recognize it. The lines stretching from the center are compass lines. One line is deeper and brighter than the others.

"That must be the line we take the heading along," says Ellen, tracing the deep line. She grabs the stone from me and places it carefully on Dad's chart, on the spot the numbers showed. Then she uses the edge of the old map to draw a line, following the deep, bright line from the stone.

"Yes, let's try it." Ellen places the stone on the same spot on the old map. She uses the edge of the other chart to draw a line out across the page.

It points past the lighthouse, past the rocks off the cliff, to a rock farther along and slightly to the left.

A rock that is only exposed at the lowest tides.

Chapter Thirteen

We don't have to talk to know that the next thing we are going to do is row as fast as we can to that rock.

Ellen grabs a compass and binoculars from the shelf. I run to the bathroom and snatch a couple of towels.

Then we're out the door and running down the path to the boat.

As we get there, Ellen shouts, "The boat's gone!"

I spin around to look, but it is nowhere to be seen.

Then I see it in the water with Joseph rowing it. "He's going toward the headland," I shout. Ellen has obviously figured that out too, because she's running as fast as she can toward the light tower. I quickly catch up with her, and the two of us hurtle over the headland. We keep to the trees. The last thing we want is for the crazy man to see us.

We top the rise and pelt down past the lighthouse to the shore below. Without even stopping to talk about it, both of us run onto the flats and head to the rocky far side of the bay. We've lived on this island all our lives. We've played on these rocks forever. We know how to get around them better than anyone.

We stop when we reach the intertidal zone. Ellen pulls out the compass.

She lines it up, then points to the spot we need to head for. We start out toward it. It's slippery and dangerous. Some of the rocks are covered in seaweed and some are still wet, so it's slow going. Ellen points out to the sea, but I've already noticed. The tide is coming in. If we don't hurry, we will be caught on the rocks.

Joseph is paddling in from the deepwater side. I keep picking my way over the rocks. Then I hear Ellen's voice from behind me, "He's seen you, Simon. He's going to try to cut you off."

I look around wildly, searching for Ellen and Joseph. Joseph is coming right at me, but he's still pretty far away. Ellen is standing at the edge of a rock, waving madly at me. She's hit a dead end. The water is too deep for her to continue.

I look back at the shore. There's a madman after me, and the tide is coming in. I take a step back. Maybe I should just wait for Mom and Dad.

Then my eyes fall upon Joseph again. He's paddling frantically toward me. I remember what this is all about. What if there really is treasure out there? Could I save the lighthouse by finding it?

Chapter Fourteen

I turn around and leap to the next rock on the right. It is hard going. Every step has to be slow and deliberate. The seaweed lying all around hides what's underneath. I almost fall into a tide pool covered completely with sea grass. I grab at the rock and pull myself forward, searching for places to put my foot. I glance back to make sure I have an escape route. If the tide comes in too fast, or if Joseph gets there first, I want to know I have a way out.

Ahead, the rock I want is still so far away. But I know I've got the right one in my sights. I step forward again, almost losing my balance. I get down on my hands and knees and crawl. Now I'm moving faster, though the rocks are hard on my knees. After about ten crawls, I reach a spot with a low surge of water between me and the next rock. I slide into the water and gasp as my feet go instantly numb. But it isn't too deep. The water pools around my knees as the tide rushes in. I take a deep breath and launch my body forward, flinging myself onto the next rock. I haul myself up to a standing position again. I turn around and wave. Ellen gives me the thumbs-up.

There is a clear path now between me and the rock with the treasure. Once again I get down on my hands and knees and crawl so I won't slip on the seaweed. My whole body is soaked by now. I inch forward. Barnacles cut my hands, my pants are heavy, my shoes are soaked and my knees ache. I crane my neck to look for Ellen, but I can't see her anymore.

The tide is coming in faster now. I take a deep breath and move forward, knowing I have to get to the rock with the treasure before waves start breaking on it. Slowly, slowly, inch by inch, I close in on it. With a stretch, I reach the next rock and pull myself up, then sit at the top and take a deep breath.

What am I looking for? It suddenly occurs to me that the treasure could have been washed away with the tide dozens of years ago. This could all be for nothing. The thought makes me so disappointed that I feel like puking. But then I look around. The rock I'm aiming for is still above water, the tide licking around its edges. As I watch, a wave comes in, darkening a patch that had dried in the sun. Hope rises in me again, and the sick feeling is replaced with excitement.

My destination is only five feet away, but the water is higher than it was even three minutes ago. A wave crashes against the rock. I consider jumping, but if I slipped on the other side, I would hit my head. So I wait until the water recedes again, then launch myself and swim the five feet through the briny water. My fingers scrabble for a hold, and I pull myself up.

I'm finally on the rock that's only visible in the lowest tide. It is barely above water now, and it's covered in purple sea stars. Through chattering teeth, I laugh as I find a small spot free of sea stars to sit on.

Here are the stars that climb out from the deep.

I made it. But the rowboat is getting closer—close enough that I can see the wildness in Joseph's eyes.

He shouts, "It's mine! I've searched all year."

I don't respond. If he thinks he can scare me away now, he's wrong.

Joseph continues. "You and your sister are pathetic. You even left your boat out for me." He laughs, and my spine tingles. He sounds like the Joker in *Batman*.

As he talks, I search with my fingers around the rock face, under the small cracks, anywhere my fingers can go.

"What did you think you would find?" I ask as I keep looking, my fingers searching frantically.

Joseph laughs again. "You don't even know. Treasure, boy, treasure beyond your imagination."

At last I feel something, and I pull.

A box the size of a man's hand emerges from a deep crack in the rock. I hug it to myself and shout, "Ellen, help!"

Joseph is almost upon me.

Chapter Fifteen

I have no time to stop and worry, no time to think about what might happen if Joseph catches up with me.

"Jump," shouts Ellen. She's ten feet away. She points to a spot I could leap to. The tide is coming in fast, and everything looks different than it did minutes ago. I have to hurry—before the tide submerges my route back to shore.

I take a deep breath, exhale and jump to the next spot that's still not submerged.

I look back. Joseph is closing in on me. He could almost reach out and grab my shirt. His face is purple with rage. He's spluttering madly at us. "You're ruining a life's work. You'll pay for this, you'll pay."

I scramble as fast as I can among the rocks in the shallows, where the boat can't go, until I reach Ellen.

"He's trying to get out of the boat!" Ellen shrieks at me. I turn and see that he's stuck. The boat is knocking hard against the rocks as the tide rushes in. Soon he manages to steady the boat and climb out. He turns toward us. He looks murderous.

I grab Ellen's arm, and together we scramble, crawl, jump and run toward shore. I keep the box clutched to my chest, ignoring how it digs into my chest every time I jump. When we reach the shoreline, Ellen says, "Don't stop. He's going to follow us. I have a plan."

She runs, circling the rocks, heading for the boat. The boat is floating closer and closer to us. Ellen leads us in a circle heading away from the boat, then turning quickly toward it so that Joseph is behind us. We are between him and the boat.

With a leap, Ellen lands on a rock and clambers over it. She lowers herself and gets her feet into the boat. She pushes off toward me, and I launch myself into the boat, nearly overturning it. I am still clutching the box. Ellen steadies the boat, and in a second we are clear of the rocks.

Ellen angles us back toward the deepest rocks, rowing wildly. Her arms pump and her hair swings with every stroke. I crane my neck around to keep track of Joseph. He's still only a few feet away. He looks like he's searching for a spot to jump into the water from. Why doesn't Ellen just row into the bay?

"What are you doing, Ellen? Row away!" I shout.

But Ellen just angles to the left and keeps rowing. Joseph changes direction again, and again comes closer. He's panting now, slipping on the rocks.

"Don't think you can get away from me!" Joseph shouts.

Ellen ignores him and keeps rowing, changing her angle again. I see what she's doing. That sister of mine is sneaky. She's pushing him farther out onto the rocks. She keeps circling, just out of his reach.

"You won't get away from me," he shouts, and he leaps into the water. But the current is strong, and he struggles against it, his arms flailing.

He shouts "It's mine!" as he lunges toward us, but again the current pushes him back. Finally he grabs at a rock and pulls himself out of the water.

"You've trapped him!" I say to Ellen.

She nods. "Yep."

I laugh and let out a huge sigh of relief.

Once the tide has risen enough that Joseph can't get off the rock, Ellen turns the boat toward our dock. She's rowing more slowly now, and her face is no longer fixed in a frown. It looks like she's trying not to grin. "He'll be fine until the coast guard arrives. That rock is always out of the water."

I flop back against the gunwale. "I can't believe it. I found something. There really was treasure. I can't believe it, treasure." I'm babbling. I can't help it. I'm frozen and exhausted, but totally one hundred and fifty percent thrilled.

Before we reach the dock, I see that two boats are tied up there. Mom and Dad are in the big motorboat, and Mark is on the coast guard boat. At last, at last! I sit up and wave and shout "Dad! Mom!" until they wave back.

"Thank goodness you're okay," Mom yells from the water. "We radioed this morning, but there was no answer. Can you believe the storm last night? The whole city was out of power, even the coast guard. I tried and tried to call."

Dad's head appears from behind the control seat. "I thought your mother was going to strangle someone when it was still stormy this morning. She was out of her mind with worry. But I kept telling her you two would be fine." He hops from the boat onto the dock and catches the lead rope I throw to him. Man, oh, man, it's good to see them.

"It looks like you two have been up to something. What's this?" Dad points to the box lying in my lap.

So we tell them. Everything. Well, we leave out the fact that we skipped some of our chores. Mom climbs out of the boat and hugs both me and Ellen. Her face turns white when we get to the part about rescuing Joseph. Dad and Mark exchange a look, but they all look interested when we finally point to the box and say, "And that's the treasure."

Dad whistles. I hold the box out for everyone to see. Mom says, "Simon, I think you should do the honors."

I grab the box to my chest and say, "On dry land, please." No way I'm taking any chances of this baby dropping in the water after all I've been through.

Now that I'm not trying to escape a madman, I take a long look at the box. It is very old, that's clear, and is made of some type of metal that has survived being under water for ages. There's a crease down the center of it, where I guess the opening is. "I...can't...open... it." I grunt as I try to pry my hands into the crease.

"Let's see." Dad takes a look. "It's been soldered shut to make it waterproof."

"Does that mean we won't be able to open it?" Ellen looks so sad, it's almost funny. But Dad shakes his head and goes back to the motorboat. He jumps on board, and a minute later he waves something in the air and hops back onto the dock and then to shore.

"I knew this would come in handy one day." He holds up a tiny crowbar. While I hold the box steady, Dad slowly, carefully, taps around the edges until the solder crumbles away.

Before I lift the lid, I look at each person in turn. Ellen's face is bright red. Mom holds her head in her hands. Dad is breathing heavily, and even Mark is staring at the box.

I lift the lid. "What is it?" says Ellen in a flat voice as I lift a circle of brass out of the box. I shake my head. I don't know. Tears sting my eyes and I blink. Until now, I didn't realize how much

I expected there to be gold or jewels in this box. But there isn't. There's just this circle of brass. Worthless. Nothing. All that chasing after Joseph for this!

I'm about to let it fall back into the box, but Dad takes it from my hands and says, "I think it's a mariner's astrolabe."

"Yeah…," I say slowly. I've heard of astrolabes, but I've never seen a real one. It hangs from Dad's hand like a huge old watch with holes. Instead of two hands inside the circle, there is only one, with points at either end.

We're all silent for a minute. Flashes of gold and silver and jewels skip through my mind. I swallow to hide my disappointment.

"How does it work?" I ask.

Dad holds the astrolabe in front of him so he is looking through one of the holes. "You line up one of the holes with the sun, then move this arm around until the sun shines through another hole, then take your reading off these notches along the side." He pushes at the arm, but it's stuck and doesn't move.

"It's broken," I say.

"Crusted in salt and water," Dad says.

"And they navigated with these?" asks Ellen.

Dad nods. "A long time ago."

Ellen steps back. "I don't get it. Why would anyone call this treasure?" She's trying to hide it, but I know Ellen's disappointed too.

Dad's face is red with excitement. "Kids, think about it. Astrolabes were used between the fifteenth and seventeenth centuries. After that they were replaced by compasses."

It takes a minute for what he's saying to sink in, but then I say, "So this could really have belonged to Juan de Fuca."

Dad nods. "Yeah, it could have."

I take the astrolabe from Dad and hold it like he had, so the light shines through it.

"You mean I could be holding something that Juan de Fuca held? I could be holding something that he used to navigate his ship along the coast of British Columbia?"

Dad nods again, and this time he grins. "You've found a real treasure, kids."

Mom's laughing and crying at the same time. Mark's just standing there with his mouth hanging open. Ellen's eyes are bulging. They all look like they've just been stunned. I bet I look the same, because I sure feel that way. I'm touching history.

A minute ago I thought this was worthless.

The thought makes me shudder, and I carefully place the astrolabe back in the box.

Dad sits down next to me. "Simon, this could mean many things, you know."

"Could it mean Juan de Fuca sailed down the strait, not just across the mouth of it?" I ask.

"It could, if the riddle is true," says Dad.

I lean into him, unable to speak.

Then Mark clears his throat. "Sorry to remind you of this, but there's still the matter of that man out on the rocks."

"You're right," says Dad, standing up. "I'll come with you. I think there'd better be two of us."

Mom, Ellen and I watch as Dad and Mark gun the boat and round out of the bay to the headland toward Joseph.

It feels like forever that we sit there watching. None of us wants to move. The tide comes in some more. I get even colder and hungrier, but all I can think about is that something huge has happened.

Chapter Sixteen

Ellen and I sleep for about a million hours. When I finally wake up, Mom is setting fresh fruit, orange juice and coffee on the breakfast table, and Dad is cooking bacon, eggs and toast.

"Good morning, Sunshine," calls Dad as I walk into the room. "How are you feeling?"

"Apart from the fact that my whole body is stiff and I have some pretty stellar bruises and cuts, I feel great. I'm starving." I have no idea when I last ate.

"Well, eat up then," says Mom.

After a huge breakfast, Ellen and I spend the day sitting around in the living room telling Mom and Dad details about our adventure. Dad frowns when we admit to missing some of our chores, but then he says, "Given the circumstances, I'm just glad you got any of them done."

One thing that's cool is that I don't mind sitting here with Ellen. It's good to have someone to share these memories with who understands what it was really like. And not once in the whole time we're talking does she give one of her looks. She doesn't contradict me or butt in when I'm explaining something. When she's talking, I watch her and think about the adventure. Ever since we saw Joseph in the water and went to rescue him, Ellen's been great. She's been fantastic. The next time she looks my way, I grin at her. She looks surprised for a second, but then she grins back.

Late in the day, the radio crackles.

"Discovery Light, Discovery Light, this is the coast guard. Over."

"This is Discovery Light. Hi, Mark. Over."

"Simon, we thought you would like to know, we contacted the Royal Historical Society and they were very glad to hear from us. It turns out, the map Joseph Edison was carrying belongs to them. He stole it sometime last year. They've been looking for him ever since. The map is extremely valuable. They want to do more research on it and on the astrolabe you found."

My heart sinks. "Does that mean we have to give the Royal Historical Society the box?"

"It means they'd like to work with you. To ask you some questions, if you're willing."

I smile. I'm willing, all right.

"So what was Joseph going to do with the box if he found it?" I ask Mark.

"He's a known dealer in stolen antiques. So I guess he would have sold it."

"Wow." The thought of how close we came to losing it makes me shiver.

"That's not why I called, Simon. We're hoping you and Ellen will testify against him. Can you do that?"

I nod, then say, "Will do, Mark. Thanks for calling. Over."

I put the radio down and walk to the window. I can see the bay and the top of the light tower. A thought that's been nagging at me all night and all morning comes to the front of my mind, and I smile. Maybe, just maybe, this adventure will be enough to convince the government to keep Discovery Lighthouse Station open.

All through the evening, friends, reporters, other lighthouse keepers and people we've never even heard of radio in and want to talk to us. Several of them say they're going to mount expeditions to find out more about Juan de Fuca's travels, to see if there are shipwrecks or other treasures to be found. Some of them invite us along, but Ellen and I say no. We've had enough adventure for a while.

Acknowledgments

Thanks to my family and to the Wildwood Writers for all the years of support.

Kari Jones is a Victoria-based writer and teacher who has a passion for the out-of-doors. She loves to spend time exploring the natural world and dreaming up adventures to share.